# Sink or Float?

Oh no! My boat is sinking!

My boat is sinking, too!

2

Look! My ball is floating.

My duck is floating, too.

Let's see what sinks!

4

Let's see what floats!

Look! These shells sink.

These rocks sink, too.

6

Look! These feathers float.

These flowers float, too.

Look! Some of my things sink.

Some of my things float.

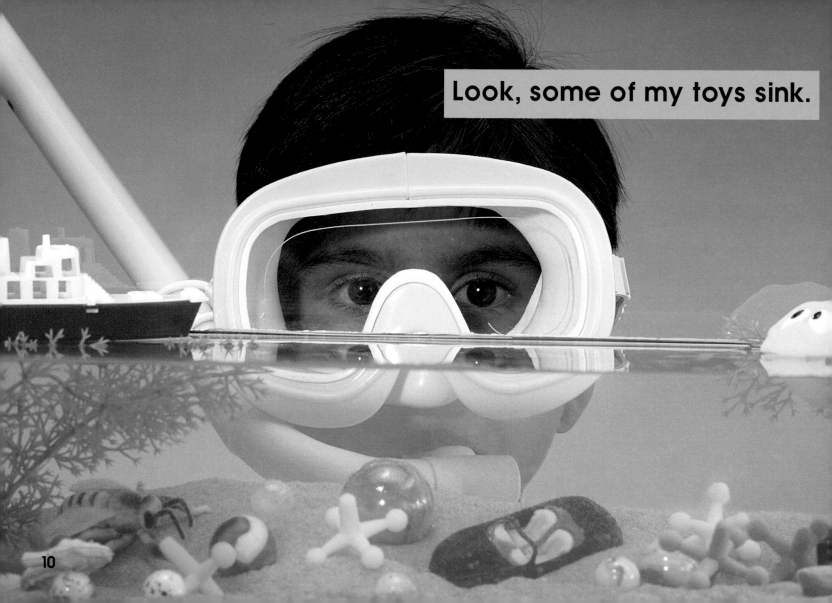

Look, some of my toys sink.

Some of my toys float.

Let's make some things sink.

Let's make some things float.

12

I can make my bottle sink.

I can make my bottle float.

13

I can make my bucket sink.

I can make my bucket float.

14

But the best thing to float is

us in a boat!